The way through the woods is dark and deep,
With many a lesson to gauge,
And the path you take is the story you make,
Each step a turn of the page.

For Katy

First published 2018 by Macmillan Children's Books
This edition published 2019 by Macmillan Children's Books
an imprint of Pan Macmillan
20 New Wharf Road, London N1 9RR
Associated companies throughout the world
www.panmacmillan.com

ISBN: 978-1-5098-1707-8

Chris Riddell

Once Upon a Wild Wood

Macmillan Children's Books

 ittle Green Rain Cape
set off through the woods.
She felt well prepared.
She had . . .

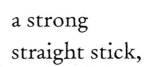 a strong
straight stick,

 comfortable
clumpy boots,

and a backpack
containing:

a good book,

breadcrumbs,

a pair of
clean socks

and an invitation
to a party.

She was wearing her green rain cape.

Green hadn't been walking for long when she met a helpful wolf.

"Can I help you?" he asked.

"No thank you," said Green.

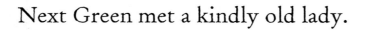

Next Green met a kindly old lady.

"Would you care for an apple?" she asked.

"No thank you," said Green.

And Green had hardly begun walking again when she met a friendly troll.

"Need directions?" he asked.

"No thank you," said Green, and she continued on her way through the woods.

Eventually she came to a castle.

"Who are you?" growled a fierce voice, as a figure with a very hairy face appeared from the rose bushes.

"My name is Little Green Rain Cape," said Green. "Are you the gardener here?"

"No, I'm a Beast," said the Beast. "Gardening is just a hobby. I don't suppose you've seen my guest, Beauty, anywhere have you? She went to visit her family and still hasn't come back. It's very lonely without her."

The Beast's eyes filled with tears.

"I'm afraid not," said Green. "But if I do, I'll tell her you're missing her."

"I am," said the Beast. "She throws sticks for me to fetch and I plait her hair with flowers. I've been invited to a party and I wanted to ask her to come with me."

And with that, he turned sadly away.

...en carried on through the woods. It began to grow dark so she looked for a place to stop for the night. She was just investigating the foot of a beanstalk when . . .

"Who are you?" asked a discarded harp that was lying on the ground.

"You can call me Green," said Green.

"Well, I'm an enchanted harp," said the harp. "I've had two simply hopeless owners. You look much more sensible. Would you like to own me?"

"I'm not sure I have room in my backpack," answered Green politely.

"No problem! You can carry me," said the harp, "and I will play for you!"

It began to rain.

"Quick!" the harp cried. "My strings will get soggy! Let's take shelter in that cave over there."

It was a very comfortable cave.

The next morning, Green was woken up by three bears.
They did not look happy.

"If my chair has been broken again, there'll be trouble,"
growled the smallest bear.

Green was about to answer when the harp piped up.

"I love what you've done with the place!" she said sweetly. "I'm
an enchanted harp. I've had *three* extremely careless owners." She
glared at Green. "The last one almost ruined my strings in the rain.
Would *you* like to own me?"

And with that, the harp began to play dance tunes for the bears,
who quickly forgot all about Green.

She crept out of the cave unnoticed.

Green continued her journey through the wild wood. Clump, clump, clump went her boots on the path.

"What a pretty cape!" said a little girl in a red cloak with a hood, stepping out suddenly from behind a tree. "But mine's prettier. And what clumpy boots! But mine are more comfortable. My grandma gave them to me. I was just telling a nice wolf all about her."

"Are you sure that was wise?" asked Green.

"I can't see why not," said the little girl, skipping off.

Green shook her head, sat down on a tree stump and took off her boots and socks.

"Aching feet?" asked a voice from a tree branch overhead. "I've got an ointment for that. Just ask the twelve dancing princesses. All that waltzing is tough on their dainty feet."

Green looked up in time to see a songbird swoop down from a nest with a tiny girl on its back.

"I'm Thumbelina," the girl said, giving Green a small jar.

"Thank you, that's so kind," said Green. She opened the jar and rubbed some of the ointment on her feet.

It felt wonderful.

Just then, a coach drew up and a prince stepped out.

"Princesses!" he exclaimed. "Did someone say princesses? Exhausting! Either falling asleep for a hundred years, losing their shoes or going out every night dancing. I was on my way to one of their parties, but I'm sure I'm coming down with something."

"Oh Prince Tarquin, you poor thing!" said Thumbelina. She whistled tunefully and several more songbirds swooped down carrying cough syrup, a silver spoon and a hot water bottle. "Now go straight home and rest," she told him.

"Excellent idea!" said Prince Tarquin hoarsely. "I'll do my best but my coach keeps breaking down. Knew I shouldn't have bought it secondhand!"

"Fairy tale problems!" sighed Thumbelina, shaking her tiny head as he drove away. "I like to do what I can to help."

"In that case," said Green, "I don't suppose that you know someone called Beauty?"

"Lovely girl!" said Thumbelina. "I've known her family for years!"

Green smiled, reached into her backpack and took out the breadcrumbs and her party invitation. "For your birds," she said. "I wonder if they might do me a favour and deliver something for me?" As the birds flew away, Green said goodbye to Thumbelina and set off again.

It wasn't long before she came to a clearing.

In the middle of the clearing was a gingerbread house, and next to the house stood three little pigs with clipboards.

"Interesting building materials," said one, tapping the walls.

"Excellent construction," said another.
The third snapped a piece off a windowsill and ate it.

"Delicious!" he said with his mouth full, "But not exactly wolf-proof."

"Should you be doing that?" asked Green.

"Probably not," said the third pig. "But then you probably shouldn't be standing on that mat." Green looked down. She was stuck fast to a toffee doormat! Just then, the door of the gingerbread house opened.

"Run for it!" squealed the three little pigs.

The witch was very short-sighted.

"Perfect!" she said, plucking Green from the toffee mat. She carried her inside and put her into a large pot. "I need some boiled greens to go with my roast dinner."

"We're not your dinner!" said the seven dwarves from a roasting tray.

"That's what you think!" cackled the witch, and she went to get some water to put in the pot.

While the witch's back was turned, Green jumped out of the pot and tiptoed over to the roasting tray. She untied the dwarves.

They picked up cake forks and made their escape.

"Crumbs!" shouted the witch.

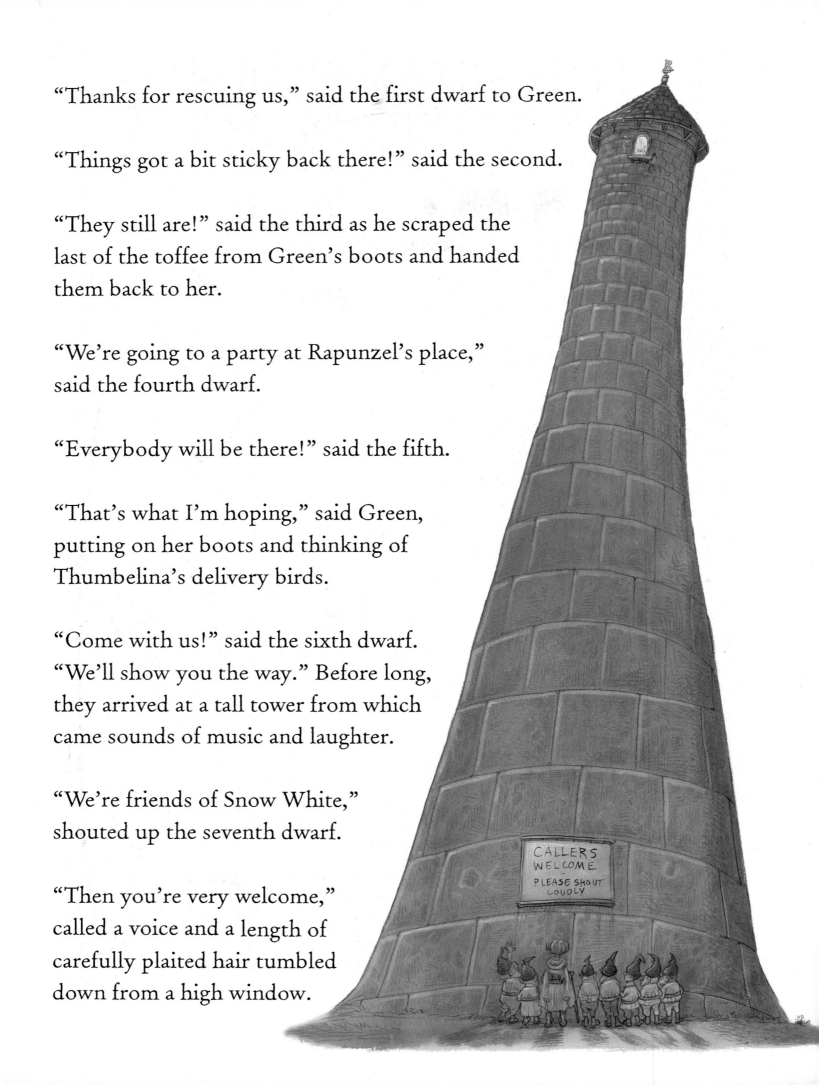

"Thanks for rescuing us," said the first dwarf to Green.

"Things got a bit sticky back there!" said the second.

"They still are!" said the third as he scraped the last of the toffee from Green's boots and handed them back to her.

"We're going to a party at Rapunzel's place," said the fourth dwarf.

"Everybody will be there!" said the fifth.

"That's what I'm hoping," said Green, putting on her boots and thinking of Thumbelina's delivery birds.

"Come with us!" said the sixth dwarf. "We'll show you the way." Before long, they arrived at a tall tower from which came sounds of music and laughter.

"We're friends of Snow White," shouted up the seventh dwarf.

"Then you're very welcome," called a voice and a length of carefully plaited hair tumbled down from a high window.

CALLERS
WELCOME

PLEASE SHOUT
LOUDLY

They all climbed up.

Rapunzel's party was great fun. The harp played everyone's favourite songs and everybody danced. Well, almost everybody.

The twelve dancing princesses took their time choosing which of the princes to dance with, while the Beast didn't seem to want to dance with anyone at all.

Until, that is, the last guest arrived . . .

Beauty flung herself into the Beast's arms.

"I'm so sorry!" she said. "I had completely lost track of time. If I'd only known how terribly lonely you were, dear Beast, I would have come back sooner."

"How did you find out?" asked the Beast, dabbing his eyes with his handkerchief. Beauty smiled as she glanced over at Thumbelina and Green.

"A little bird told me,"
she replied.

The party continued all night long.

The twelve dancing princesses had made up their minds and were wearing out their dancing shoes.

Rapunzel used her hair as a skipping rope and everyone took turns to skip in time to the harp's music.

Little Red Riding Hood danced a show-stopping tango with the wolf,

while the three little pigs led the line dancing,

and the troll and the kindly old lady got to know each other.

Everyone had a wonderful time . . .

. . . especially Beauty and the Beast.

The next morning, Green woke up early. She put on her rain cape and picked up her backpack, but not her strong straight stick, which she had given to the Beast as a present.

Then, as the sun began to rise, she slipped away.

"I wonder," thought Green to herself as she continued on her way through the wild wood, "what will happen next . . ."

For the way through the woods is dark and deep,
With many a lesson to gauge,
And the path you take is the story you make,
Each step a turn of the page.